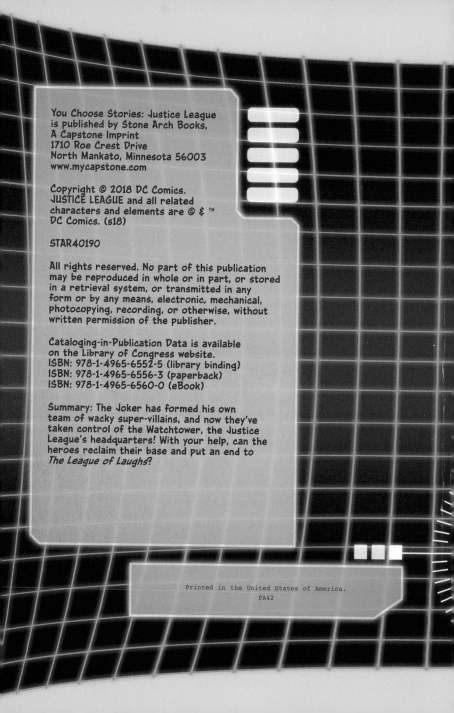

You Choose Stories: Justice League
is published by Stone Arch Books,
A Capstone Imprint
1710 Roe Crest Drive
North Mankato, Minnesota 56003
www.mycapstone.com

STAR40190

Cataloging-in-Publication Data is available
on the Library of Congress website.
ISBN: 978-1-4965-6552-5 (library binding)
ISBN: 978-1-4965-6556-3 (paperback)
ISBN: 978-1-4965-6560-0 (eBook)

Summary: The Joker has formed his own
team of wacky super-villains, and now they've
taken control of the Watchtower, the Justice
League's headquarters! With your help, can the
heroes reclaim their base and put an end to
The League of Laughs?

Printed in the United States of America.
PA42

DC SUPER HEROES

←YOU CHOOSE→

JUSTICE LEAGUE™

THE LEAGUE OF LAUGHS

written by
Matthew K. Manning

illustrated by
Erik Doescher

STONE ARCH BOOKS
a capstone imprint

THE LEAGUE
OF LAUGHS

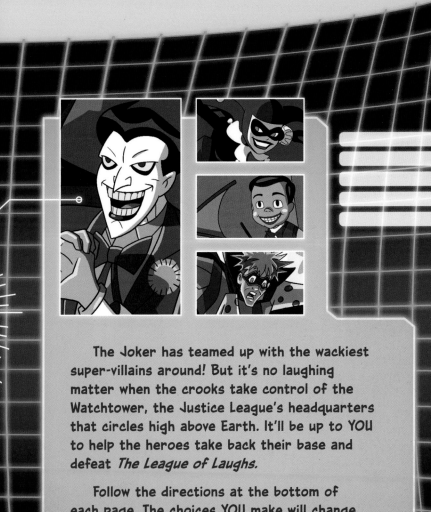

The Joker has teamed up with the wackiest super-villains around! But it's no laughing matter when the crooks take control of the Watchtower, the Justice League's headquarters that circles high above Earth. It'll be up to YOU to help the heroes take back their base and defeat *The League of Laughs.*

Follow the directions at the bottom of each page. The choices YOU make will change the outcome of the story. After you finish one path, go back and read the others for more Justice League adventures!

Batman sits alone in the Justice League's monitor room aboard the Watchtower.

As usual, the large chamber is dark. The only light comes from a few dozen monitors in front of the hero. The screens glow as they switch from live 24-hour news to city security cameras, then to satellite images of peaceful countryside.

Batman studies the screens carefully. He's one of the only Justice League members without superpowers, but the Dark Knight is more than capable of watching every monitor. Unlike some of the Justice League's younger members, Batman realizes just how serious his job is.

"Hello, Clark," Batman says, breaking the shadowy silence.

"Didn't think you heard me come in," replies Superman as he steps farther into the room.

Turn the page.

"You know me better than that," says Batman.

Indeed, Superman does know his teammate better than that. He knows him better than anyone else in the Justice League.

Years ago, Batman used his detective skills to figure out that Superman is newspaper reporter Clark Kent. Meanwhile, Superman only had to use his X-ray vision to discover that Batman was billionaire Bruce Wayne.

Not many people are aware of Batman's secret identity, so Superman considers the knowledge an honor. When it comes to Batman, knowing any of his secrets is an achievement.

"I guess I do, Bruce," says Superman. "Is it just us on monitor duty tonight?"

"Cyborg should be here soon," says Batman. His eyes stay focused on the monitors. "He just finished stopping a global group of computer hackers. It took him less than an hour."

"For the new guy, Cyborg is doing pretty well," says Superman.

"He wouldn't still be here if he couldn't keep up," says Batman.

"You're all heart, Bruce," jokes Superman.

Batman smiles. Just slightly. Superman certainly does know him.

Batman stands up from the chair. He stretches his back, and then finally turns away from the monitors.

He says, "I've got a case I need to get back to in Gotham City if—"

"Wait," says Superman.

Batman stops. If Superman is cutting him off mid-sentence, there's a good reason for it.

The Man of Steel frowns. "Did you hear that?"

"No," replies Batman. "You're the only one here with super-hearing."

"It . . . ," Superman starts to say. His eyebrows lower. "It sounded like . . . laughter."

Turn the page.

KABOOOM!!!

Something tears through the outside wall of the Watchtower.

Superman barely has time to turn around when he's hit in the gut. A red blur plows into the hero with the speed and power of a semitruck on the highway. Superman crashes into the opposite wall. He misses Batman by less than a foot.

It doesn't take Superman long to realize who this blur is.

Batman recognizes him too. "Bizarro," he says under his breath.

Bizarro is a powerhouse in a cape and Superman's imperfect clone. The villain has nearly the same powers as the hero. It had been nothing for Bizarro to burst through the armored hull of the Watchtower satellite.

Now the gaping hole is causing chaos. Batman holds on tight to a desk as the vacuum of space tugs and pulls at his body.

As Superman wrestles with Bizarro, Batman knows the hole needs to be fixed—and fast. All the breathable air is being sucked out of the satellite. He looks over at the destroyed wall.

Just then a huge, toy-like robot flies into the wrecked room. Rockets on its metal body boost it inside.

Clunk!

The robot lands heavily on the floor. It appears Bizarro isn't working alone.

The giant robot fires a beam at the hole in the wall. Batman's legs hit the ground. The gravity is back to normal. The robot has sealed the opening with some sort of high-tech force field.

A panel opens on the robot's chest. Batman's eyes narrow. Now everything makes sense.

Out of the robot walks the deadliest enemy the Dark Knight has ever faced. He could recognize that pale face and green hair anywhere.

"The Joker," Batman grumbles.

Turn the page.

"Last stop," yells the Joker in his best conductor voice. "End of the line, League of Laughs."

As Superman and Bizarro tumble through the room, Batman's hand goes to his Utility Belt. But he crouches behind the desk and waits. He needs to know who he's up against before he acts.

Batman watches the Joker's girlfriend, Harley Quinn, somersault out of the robot. Behind her is Trickster, a gimmick-crazed enemy of the super-speeding hero known as The Flash.

The last villain is Toyman, but he comes as no surprise to Batman. Like Bizarro, Toyman is another of Superman's foes. The mask-wearing criminal is obsessed with making deadly versions of everyday children's toys. The toy-like robot ship is obviously one of his creations.

"Don't tell me," says the Joker as the villains walk around the destroyed room. "Did we take the wrong turn at Albuquerque?"

The Joker turns and looks right at the Dark Knight. But the clown is the only one smiling.

One hour later, the Watchtower's teleporter buzzes to life.

Cyborg steps out of the machine and cracks his metal knuckles. It's an old habit from before the accident. To save his life, he had been given mechanical parts. The parts had also changed him into half man, half machine super hero.

"Hey, Batman," he says as he walks into the monitor room. "I'm here, reporting for—"

Then Cyborg notices the giant patched hole in the wall. And the room is completely wrecked.

Cyborg's electronic pulse quickens. His teammates were supposed to be here, but there's no Dark Knight. No Man of Steel.

But he finds something else. A purple smile is spray-painted on the wall. Below it, someone's written the words *LEAGUE OF LAUGHS*.

Cyborg exhales. This isn't how he saw the night going.

If Cyborg searches for Batman, turn to page 14.
If Cyborg looks for Superman, turn to page 18.
If Cyborg leaves the Watchtower, turn to page 17.

There's no time to panic. Cyborg needs to find Batman. The Dark Knight is one of the smartest heroes around. He's sure to have a plan for fighting off this super-villain invasion.

But in order to find Batman, first Cyborg has to figure out what happened.

He types on a keyboard near the monitors. The room is heavily damaged, but at least the computers are still working. Cyborg plays back the security video from the monitor room.

Images flash by. Bizarro attacks Superman. Toyman's robot enters the Watchtower, and the Joker and his teammates exit the toy-like ship. Then Superman knocks Bizarro out of the monitor room and flies into the hall. He leaves the sight of the security camera.

Cyborg rewinds the video to watch it again. He can see Batman in a dark corner of the room. The Joker and the Dark Knight even seem to exchange a few words. But then Batman throws down a smoke bomb.

Just like that, he disappears.

"OK, Batman. So where did you go?" Cyborg says to himself.

He begins to type more commands. He needs to pull up the security videos from the hallway cameras to learn more. But before Cyborg finishes, a jolt of electricity pulses through his body.

ZZZZZAAAAPPPPPP!!!

"See, I told you he was a real live boy," says the high-pitched voice of Harley Quinn.

Cyborg looks up from his new position on the ground. Harley and Trickster stand over him. The joy buzzer in Trickster's hand is still smoking.

"Huh," says Trickster. "And here I thought he was just some sort of robot butler."

Cyborg grits his teeth. The time for gathering info is over. It's time to act.

If Cyborg attacks Trickster and Harley, turn to page 21.
If Cyborg tries to talk to the criminals, turn to page 27.

Cyborg thinks it over. Superman and Batman have to be down for the count. A group of super-villains must've taken over the Watchtower. There's no other explanation.

That leaves Cyborg with only one choice. He needs to get out of the satellite and find help. Sending more power to his legs, he runs down the hallway, back to the teleportation room.

In the room stand several teleporters. They've all been newly remodeled and should be working perfectly.

Cyborg steps onto a teleporter and focuses. His robotic mind can talk with almost any type of computer. With a simple thought, he powers up the machine.

But then he realizes something. If he can still connect to the teleporters, that means he can probably still link up with the rest of the Watchtower's systems.

Maybe leaving the Watchtower isn't the best course of action after all.

If Cyborg stays on the Watchtower, turn to page 23.
If Cyborg teleports to Earth, turn to page 29.

There's no doubt in Cyborg's mind. If he wants to know what happened, he has to find the heart of the Justice League. He has to track down Superman.

Cyborg walks over to one of the computer consoles. The tip of his finger flips open to reveal a USB stick. Cyborg presses it into a port on the main console.

Nothing appears on the screen. But it doesn't have to. Cyborg sees everything inside his mind.

The security videos flash through his brain in half a second. The Joker and a group of villains break into the Watchtower. Bizarro knocks Superman into another room, and the others gang up on Batman. Cyborg watches as Harley Quinn whacks the hero with her oversized mallet. Then Trickster tosses a bomb. It explodes with foam that covers Batman. The material hardens, completely trapping him.

It's clear that the Dark Knight has become the Joker's prisoner, but what about the Man of Steel? Cyborg scrolls through the images.

"Booyah," he says under his breath.

He's found more security camera video. The camera in the Watchtower's gym recorded a bit of Superman's fight with his imperfect clone. And from the looks of the Watchtower's sensor records, there was also some kind of activity in the storage area on the satellite's lowest level. But the camera was destroyed before anyone entered its frame.

BRAAAAMP BRAAAAMP BRAAAAMP

Cyborg stops reviewing the Watchtower data and snaps back to reality. The monitors in front of him are flashing red as they sound a warning signal.

Something set off another security alarm. This one is coming from the training room. Cyborg needs to make a decision.

Which place should he investigate?

If Cyborg heads to the gym, turn to page 25.
If Cyborg checks the lowest level, turn to page 32.
If Cyborg goes to the training room, turn to page 48.

Cyborg doesn't hesitate. With a simple thought, his metal wrist flips open. Inside is a high-tech stun gun. He zaps the metal panel upon which Trickster and Harley stand.

FZZZAAAACCCCKKKK!!!

Electricity surges through the metal panel and into the villains. Cyborg gets to his feet as Harley Quinn and Trickster fall to the floor.

The two criminal clowns didn't expect the hero to fight fire with fire. Or in this case, to fight wattage with wattage. That jolt should have them out for at least an hour.

"It's not going to be that easy with the others," says a raspy voice.

Cyborg turns to see Batman stepping out of the shadows in the hallway.

"It's never easy with the Joker," the Dark Knight says.

Turn the page.

"Batman! Where's Superman?" Cyborg asks.

He walks over toward his teammate. It's hard to see the Dark Knight clearly. He's sulking in the shadows like usual. Cyborg briefly thinks about turning on his night vision just to see the hero better.

"He took his fight with Bizarro outside," says Batman. "Knowing Superman, they're in another solar system by now."

"So that just leaves Toyman," says Cyborg.

"And the Joker," adds Batman.

The closer Cyborg gets, the more the Dark Knight steps back into the darkness. His teammate is being even more mysterious than usual. It's as if Batman still doesn't trust Cyborg as a fellow Justice League member.

"But I know where they're hiding," says Batman. "Follow me."

If Cyborg goes with Batman, turn to page 34.
If Cyborg stays put, turn to page 52.

Cyborg steps out of the teleporter. He made a mistake.

Getting backup will take time, but Superman's and Batman's lives are in danger now. If Cyborg can connect to the Watchtower's systems, he might be able to help them.

The hero heads out into the hall. He blinks, and his vision changes. He no longer sees the metal walls and floors of the Watchtower. As he walks, he now sees a digital image of the satellite's blueprints on top of the real world structure.

After a few minutes, Cyborg stops and looks to the left. He's found what he was searching for—a small control panel in the wall. His metal fingers grip the edge of the panel's cover, and he flips it open.

"Aw, puddin', c'mon!" a shrill voice sounds from around a corner. It's Harley Quinn.

Cyborg needs to work faster.

Turn the page.

Behind the cover is a USB port. The tip of Cyborg's finger flips open and reveals his own USB drive.

He plugs into the port. Suddenly, a large panel slides open in the wall. The entrance had been invisible just moments before.

"That's enough, Harley," says the Joker.

The voices are closer now. It sounds like they're about to turn the corner.

Cyborg slaps the panel cover closed and ducks into the large opening. The door slides shut. The hero looks around. He's in a maintenance closet. It's one of many built to make sure the Watchtower runs smoothly.

Cyborg presses his ear against the closed door. It sounds like the Joker is right outside.

"If you knock off Batman and Superman, then the joke is ruined," says the Joker. "Humor comes in threes, you know."

If Cyborg leaps out to attack the Joker and Harley, turn to page 36.

If Cyborg stays hidden in the maintenance closet, turn to page 55.

When Cyborg steps into the gym, the room is totally dark.

"Lights," he says.

The Watchtower's systems are supposed to be voice activated. But the lights don't turn on.

Cyborg spends a second trying to remotely tap into the Watchtower's lighting system, but the Wi-Fi is down. The hero scowls.

"Great," he mutters.

He blinks his electronic eye. The room instantly fills with an eerie green light. Cyborg has switched his systems over to night vision.

He scans the room before going any farther. Something doesn't feel quite right, and he doesn't want to walk right into a trap.

Cyborg doesn't spot anything. He just sees treadmills, large pressure devices that can challenge even Superman's strength, free weights, and high-intensity elliptical machines.

It's nothing out of the ordinary.

Turn the page.

Cyborg steps toward the boxing ring at the center of the gym. A piercing white light suddenly fills the room. He blinks his eye to return to normal vision, but it's too late. The brilliant flash has briefly blinded him.

WHACK!

A large fist smacks into Cyborg's metal torso and sends him flying. He hits the wall hard. As he stands up, he gets a good look at his opponent. It's Toyman's enormous robot ship.

The hero groans. "I knew it was a trap."

Then the giant robot shudders, and Cyborg discovers the fight is only just getting started.

Toyman's robot is breaking apart. It splits into five sections, like one of the toys from Cyborg's childhood. Each part is transforming into a large robotic animal.

Cyborg stares at his five new foes. He's not sure he has time to battle mechanical beasts.

If Cyborg fights the robot animals, turn to page 68.
If Cyborg runs and continues his hunt for Superman, turn to page 86.

"What . . . what do you want?" asks Cyborg weakly from the floor.

"Gee, lemme think about it," says Harley as Trickster kicks the hero while he's down.

"Ah!" Trickster yells. The kick hurt his foot more than it did Cyborg's metal torso.

"What would a bunch of clowns and a guy obsessed with gizmos for kids want with the Justice League's Watchtower?" Harley says.

She raises an oversized mallet and steadies it at Cyborg, like a baseball player getting ready to swing.

Cyborg tries to get to his feet, but he's still feeling the jolt of electricity from Trickster's original attack. His systems need a few more seconds to fully reboot.

Harley grins. "We want your toys."

And then she swings her mallet.

Turn the page.

When Cyborg slowly opens his eyes, the first thing he notices is his splitting headache. Harley must've whacked him so hard that he passed out.

The second thing Cyborg notices is that he's now in a Watchtower cell. The Justice League designed the prison to hold even the most powerful villains.

But no criminals are locked up in it today. Only heroes.

Because the final thing Cyborg spots is both Batman and Superman lying unconscious in separate cells next to his. A painted green smile glows on Superman's chest. Cyborg's guess is that the green stuff is liquid Kryptonite.

The hero looks around the rest of the room. There's no sign of Harley, Trickster, or any of the other League of Laughs members.

If he's going to act, now's the time.

If Cyborg tries to wake Batman, turn to page 70.
If Cyborg tries to break out of his cell, turn to page 89.

Cyborg realizes he has to stop second-guessing himself. The hero activates the teleporter. Within seconds, he feels a gentle buzzing throughout his body.

When it ends, Cyborg is back on Earth and standing in a dirty city alley. He's not sure exactly where he's been placed. He didn't have time to check the teleporter's coordinates. He needed to get out of the Watchtower as quickly as possible.

"Cyborg," says a familiar voice. "This is an unexpected surprise."

Cyborg spins around to see a raven-haired woman standing in the shadows.

He recognizes her right away. It's Huntress, one of the Justice League's best fighters and an expert with a crossbow.

"I think you're blocking my teleporter," Huntress says.

Turn the page.

"The Watchtower," Cyborg begins. His voice sounds more panicked than he realizes. "It's been—"

"Taken over by the League of Laughs," says Huntress. "Or whatever the Joker is calling his group of nut jobs."

"How did you—" Cyborg starts to ask.

"Batman," Huntress interrupts again.

Cyborg nods. That's the only explanation he needs.

But Huntress continues anyway. "He managed to send out a distress call to all active Justice League members. I was on my way to the Watchtower now."

"I'm not sure that's a good idea," says Cyborg.

"Sounds like the rookie is bailing on his team," Huntress says with a smirk. "Come on, we need to go."

If Cyborg returns to the Watchtower with Huntress, turn to page 72.

If Cyborg convinces Huntress to stay on Earth, turn to page 92.

Cyborg carefully moves through the shadowy halls of the Watchtower's lowest level. He can already hear voices coming from one of the storage rooms. He crouches down into a dark corner and listens.

"So how are you different from my puddin'?" Harley Quinn asks Trickster as they search the large storage room.

Trickster sighs. "What? I don't understand the question. Can we please just focus on the job? The Joker wants us to look for anything on this floor that might be worth taking. Let's concentrate on doing that."

"I mean, you're kinda like the knockoff brand, you know?" Harley continues anyway. "A copycat, some might say."

Trickster looks away from his flashlight's beam and into the eyes of this crazy woman wearing black and red.

"Are you saying I'm just ripping off the Joker's shtick?" Trickster asks.

"Some were saying that," says Harley. "Yup."

"Are you one of that 'some'?" Trickster asks.

"I might have brought up the subject," says Harley. "But it was only outta brand loyalty, you understand."

"I don't understand half of what comes out of your mouth!" says Trickster.

He would continue to yell at her, but a pulse of sound suddenly smacks into him like a fist.

WEEEEOOOOOOOOOOO!!!

"Ungh!" Trickster cries as he's knocked to the floor.

"See," says Harley, looking down at her blacked-out teammate. "You can't even do a decent slip-and-fall. Good thing you signed up with Mr. J. He's got a lot to learn ya."

Turn to page 39.

Cyborg follows Batman into the shadowy hallway. "The lights are out," he says. "Not a good sign."

"Watchtower electrical systems have been spotty since the League of Laughs invaded," replies Batman.

The Dark Knight walks at least fifty feet in front of Cyborg. It's as if he doesn't even want to share the same hallway as the new Justice League member.

"So, how have you avoided capture this whole time?" asks Cyborg.

Batman ignores the question. "In here," he says instead, stopping at a locked door. "The Joker and Toyman are holed up in the Trophy Room."

Cyborg finally catches up to the Dark Knight. As he does, Batman steps to the side. He hides himself in the heaviest shadows of the dark hall.

"Kind of taking this whole 'creature of the night' thing a bit far, aren't you?" Cyborg says.

The Dark Knight stays silent, and Cyborg immediately regrets the joke. Batman doesn't seem to like his humor.

"I need you to open the door," continues Batman. "My access code isn't working."

Cyborg looks at the shadowy figure. "Yeah," he says. "OK."

The half man, half machine hero types a few numbers into the control panel to the right of the door.

"Access denied," the system says.

"Huh," Cyborg says. "My code isn't working either."

"What?" says Batman. He sounds impatient. "What do you mean it isn't working?"

"The Joker's crew must have locked me out, same as they did for you," replies Cyborg.

Batman doesn't say anything.

Turn to page 42.

"Booyah!" Cyborg shouts as the closet's hidden door opens. He leaps in front of the Joker and Harley Quinn.

He wishes he had time to think up a better opening line, but he's still new at this whole Justice League thing. He aims his white sound cannon at the two villains.

"Don't move!" he adds.

"Look, Harl!" the Joker says, his smile widening. "Now if that's not comedic timing, I don't know what is!"

Cyborg stares at the Joker. He has no idea what the madman is talking about. The Joker doesn't seem very concerned that Cyborg's cannon is pointed directly at his face.

In fact, the Joker seems happy about it.

Harley looks puzzled. "I don't get it, Mr. J?"

The Joker shakes his head. "You have so much to learn."

"Hey! I said, don't move!" Cyborg shouts.

"Who?" asks the Joker. He points. "Me, or the guy behind you?"

Cyborg doesn't turn around. He's new at the super hero game, but he's not *that* new. Instead, his mind instantly switches to his external sensors. They'll be able to pick up anything unusual. Cyborg focuses the sensors on the area behind him.

The Joker isn't bluffing. Bizarro is zooming right for him!

The half-metal hero tries to turn and attack, but he's not fast enough.

WHUMP!

Bizarro collides with Cyborg and sends the hero flying down the hallway. The Joker and Harley barely have time to step out of the way.

CRRRRRRUUUUNK!

Cyborg crashes into the wall, and everything goes dark.

Turn to page 45.

WEEEEOOOOOOOOOOO!!!

Thanks to years of practice on monkey bars and trampolines, Harley Quinn easily jumps over the next blast of white sound from Cyborg's arm cannon. She lands perfectly and raises her arms like a gymnast.

"Ta-da!" she says with a smile. But Harley rarely does anything without a smile.

"Don't move, Quinn," says Cyborg as he steps out of the shadows. He points his cannon straight at the villain.

"Ren row ran ri ralk?" Harley says through clenched teeth and unmoving lips.

Cyborg blinks. "What?"

"Then how can I talk?" Harley says again, clearer this time. She's already given up on her joke.

"Oopsie. I moved, didn't I? I really gotta learn more self-control," Harley adds, leaping into the air. She starts to pull something out from behind her back.

Turn the page.

Cyborg snaps into high alert. Harley could be reaching for anything. A gun. A knife. Something worse. He fires a quick blast from his white sound cannon.

WEEEOOO!

The powerful force knocks her out of the air like an excited puppy snatching a Frisbee. When he's sure she's down for the count, Cyborg walks over. In Harley's hand is a raw fish. That was her weapon of choice.

Cyborg sighs as he takes out a pair of handcuffs stored in the side of his metal thigh. He cuffs Trickster and Harley together and then heads to the exit. He's halfway there when the heavy metal doors slam shut.

FSSSSSSSSSSSSSSSSS

Cyborg looks up at the vent near the door. A thick green gas is pouring into the room. As if by instinct, a mask pops out of his chest. It covers the lower half of his face, protecting him from the mysterious gas.

"Where do you get all those wonderful toys?" says the Joker's voice, booming through the Watchtower's loudspeaker.

Cyborg isn't listening. He's trying to connect to the Watchtower's computer systems. But it isn't working. The Joker must've locked him out. And the metal doors are too tough for even Cyborg to break through.

"How long does the filter in one of those mask things last?" says the Joker, laughing to himself. "Because I've got all day!"

Cyborg checks the power. It's at four percent. He hasn't had time to recharge since the last case. The hero looks at Harley and Trickster. The Joker is gassing his own people just to get to him.

Suddenly, Cyborg's mind becomes cloudy. The Joker Venom gas is already in his system.

He doesn't want to, but he can't help but let out a chuckle. And if help doesn't come soon, Cyborg might never stop laughing. . . .

THE END

To follow another path, turn to page 13.

"Try your code again," Batman finally says.

"Yeah," says Cyborg. "Maybe I just entered it wrong."

He turns back to the control panel and begins to type.

"Now it's working!" Cyborg says. "Oh, wait. It's saying I need a ranking Justice League member to confirm my entry code."

"To confirm," says Batman. His voice sounds unsure, which is unusual for the Dark Knight.

"Yeah, the confirmation code is 1-9-8-0," says Cyborg. "The system just needs a different heat signature to type it in, I guess. Probably because I'm so new."

Batman steps in front of Cyborg. He reaches for the panel.

But his hand never touches it. Because that's the exact moment that Cyborg strikes Batman in the back of the head.

The Dark Knight crumples to the ground. But he doesn't fall like a human being. He collapses like a piece of broken machinery.

Because that's exactly what he is. This isn't the Dark Knight at all. It's a lifelike Batman robot, no doubt created by Toyman.

Cyborg had figured it out as soon as the two stepped into the hallway. When his system ran a simple scan for new threats, he hadn't picked up his teammate's heartbeat. Blocking that sound from Cyborg's sensors would be a trick even the real Batman would find difficult to pull off.

But Cyborg followed the robot just the same. He wanted to see what the imposter was up to.

Now Cyborg crouches next to the machine. He scans the broken "toy" with a sensor in his left palm. A remote-control signal is coming from the third-floor observation deck.

Toyman must be there. That's where he's pulling the robot's strings. So that's where Cyborg needs to go.

Turn the page.

"I'm telling you, something is wrong," says Toyman to the Joker. "I'm not getting a signal from my robot Batman."

The Joker steps away from the impressive view of the observation deck. He's not interested in staring out into space or looking at Earth. He's interested in what's inside the Watchtower.

The only reason he pulled together the League of Laughs was to rob the Justice League's Trophy Room. The League keeps a treasure trove of alien weapons there. The Joker can barely imagine all the fun he could have with that tech.

Unfortunately, things so far haven't gone quite as planned.

"More problems, Joker?" says Batman. "You've already lost track of Superman and Bizarro."

It's hard for the hero to talk from his position on the floor. Trickster trapped him in a thick hardening foam right after the villains had invaded. But Batman speaks just the same.

Turn to page 64.

"Ugh . . . ," Cyborg groans as he wakes up. Bizarro must've knocked him out in the hallway. His body hurts all over.

It takes a second for his vision to clear. High-tech shackles on his wrists and ankles chain him to a wall. It's hard to see anything else, though. His electronic eye seems to be a bit cracked.

"How was your nap?" a voice asks.

The hero doesn't recognize it at first. He looks up, holding back another groan as he moves his sore neck.

Trickster stands in front of him. Behind the villain are even more criminals. The Joker, Harley Quinn, Toyman, and Bizarro are all lounging around the Watchtower's monitor room.

Cyborg focuses on Toyman. He's the only one who seems busy out of the entire League of Laughs. He's typing commands into the satellite's navigation system.

Turn the page.

"It's worse than it looks," says a voice to Cyborg's side.

The hero turns and sees Batman. He's covered in some kind of hardened foam. Next to the Dark Knight lies an unconscious Superman.

"Are we ready, Freddie?" the Joker asks, slapping Toyman's back.

"Why can't you get my name correct, Joker?" asks Toyman from behind his creepy, doll-like mask. He presses a button. "But yes, I'm ready."

"Then put a smile on this place!" the Joker says. He breaks out into crazed laughter.

BOOM! BOOM! BOOM!

Cyborg quickly checks his systems. Bizarro did a lot of damage, but he can still tap into a few security videos outside the Watchtower. He pulls up the footage from near where those explosions sounded.

"He . . . ," Cyborg says to Batman. "He . . ."

"Fashioned the Watchtower in his own image," finishes Batman.

Unlike Cyborg, the Dark Knight can't see the smile that's just been carved into the Watchtower by the explosions. But Batman doesn't need to see it. He knows the Joker's twisted mind well.

"After all these years of partnering with bozos, I've finally found the right set of clowns," the Joker says. "And every good team needs a hideout."

"So you took ours," Cyborg says.

"Oh, don't sound so depressed," says the Joker. "You three stooges will get a front-row seat for all the fun to come."

Cyborg lowers his head in defeat. He hopes the rest of the Justice League has better luck beating the villains. But for now, he does his best to ignore the Joker's laughter.

THE END

To follow another path, turn to page 13.

Cyborg knows the site of the most recent security alarm is the best place to start. He must investigate the training room.

Cyborg runs over to the elevator and presses the down button. It doesn't light up.

The Watchtower's electrical systems seem to be flickering in and out. Cyborg groans. This is no doubt another one of the League of Laughs' "jokes."

Sending more of his body's electrical power to his arms with just a thought, Cyborg pulls the elevator doors open. He looks down the dark, empty shaft. Then he looks up and sees the elevator car frozen in place a few floors above. The training room is two stories below where Cyborg is now.

"How do I get down to the training room?" he mutters to himself.

Cyborg thinks for a moment and decides the direct route would also be the quickest.

So he steps into the empty elevator shaft.

Cyborg falls, but he's ready.

As he hurtles downward, Cyborg points his right hand at a nearby ledge and concentrates. The hand rockets off his wrist. But even as the hand shoots up and away, it's still connected to Cyborg by a thin, incredibly tough cord.

The hand grabs the ledge, and the cord goes tight. Just like that, Cyborg isn't falling any longer. He hangs in the elevator shaft, a few floors below the training room.

Cyborg narrows his eyes and focuses. The cord starts to reel back into his arm. He's pulled up toward the floor with the training room.

As he gets closer, a sound starts to echo through the metal chamber.

HUUUUUUMMMMMMMMMMMM

Cyborg looks up, but he already knows what's happening.

The Watchtower's elevator has powered back on. And the elevator car is plunging toward him at a ferocious speed.

Turn the page.

Cyborg sends more of his interior power to his arm. The cord reels in faster.

The hero doesn't bother to look at the elevator car speeding toward him. It'll do nothing but distract him from what needs to be done.

Right as he reaches the floor of the training room, Cyborg aims a powerful kick at the elevator door. The metal buckles and bursts outward.

Cyborg swings himself out of the shaft just as the elevator car rushes past.

WHOOOOOOSH!

It misses his head by inches.

Cyborg sits on the training room floor and gives himself a moment to breathe. That was closer than he had planned.

Turn to page 58.

Cyborg doesn't move. Something is definitely off with his teammate.

"So, where are the Joker and Toyman?" Cyborg asks.

"They're in the Trophy Room. They're after the weapons and tech that's stored there," says Batman.

"Oh," says Cyborg. His mind is racing. "How did you find all that out?"

"I've been biding my time," says Batman. "Waiting for the right opportunity."

Cyborg frowns. That didn't really answer his question. "What's the plan now?"

"We take the fight to them," Batman replies.

"The best way to do that," says Cyborg, "would be to cut off the Watchtower security systems. That'll make it easier for us to get inside the locked Trophy Room. I can do that from here in the monitor room."

"All right," says Batman. He's still hiding in the shadows. "That should work."

Cyborg moves toward the monitor room's control panels. Then a switch suddenly pops out of the back of his hand.

"Wait, is that—" Batman starts to say. But before he can finish, Cyborg flips the switch.

VVVVVOOOOOOOOMMM

A low hum fills the chamber. Batman collapses to the ground.

"Yeah," says Cyborg, walking over to the unconscious figure. "That was an electromagnetic pulse. It takes out all nearby electronic devices. Except my own, of course."

Cyborg reaches down and taps his knuckles on the Dark Knight's head. Sparks and smoke fly out.

Just as the hero expected, this isn't Batman at all. It's a robot, one undoubtedly built by Toyman.

Turn the page.

As Cyborg is about to stand and walk away, a familiar voice fills the room. It's being broadcast from a radio in the robot Batman's head.

"Well, aren't you a spoilsport," says the voice. "Do you know how long Toyboy worked on that?"

"It's *Toyman*," corrects another voice through the radio.

"You're not fooling anyone, Timmy," says the first voice. It doesn't take a Dark Knight detective to piece together who's speaking. The Joker's crazed voice is easy to recognize.

"My name's not—" the other voice continues.

FZZZZZAAAACCKKK

"Sorry about that, folks," says the Joker. "Little Timmy needed to go night-night."

Cyborg shakes his head. The Joker has just taken out his last teammate. Now it's one against one. This clown is certainly the most unpredictable villain in the Justice League's database.

Turn to page 62.

It takes every ounce of his self-control, but Cyborg stays hidden inside the secret maintenance closet.

If he's going to beat the League of Laughs, he'll need to use more than his fists. He'll need to use his brains.

Cyborg waits until he can no longer hear the Joker and Harley Quinn in the hallway. Then he gets to work.

The closet is full of advanced, high-tech equipment. It's one of the reasons that it's hidden so well. If Cyborg hadn't brought up the Watchtower's blueprints, he would never have guessed how important the maintenance rooms truly are.

Once again, Cyborg plugs into a USB port. Millions of ones and zeroes flash through his mind as he taps into the satellite's computer systems.

Turn the page.

After a full three minutes, the process is complete. Cyborg's systems are totally connected to those of the Watchtower.

Cyborg turns toward the closed panel in the wall. He doesn't have to plug into a control panel now. He just thinks the command, and the door opens instantly.

Cyborg steps out into the hall. He knows it's empty before he even looks around.

The Watchtower's sensors are online, and Cyborg has full access to every system in the satellite. With a thought, he knows where his targets are.

Trickster sits with Bizarro in the cafeteria. Cyborg can see them on the security camera. Trickster laughs as he watches the Superman clone chow down. The Joker and Harley are heading toward the monitor room. Toyman is already there, busy typing commands into the Watchtower's navigation system.

Cyborg begins to walk toward the monitor room. It's the only option. Because he can also see that's where the League of Laughs are keeping Batman and Superman.

As he moves, Cyborg shuts off every security camera and sensor in his path. He doesn't want Toyman to know he's coming.

In his mind, the robotic hero studies the monitor room closely. Batman is unconscious and covered in hardened foam. Superman has also been knocked out.

The Man of Steel's wrists are chained by glowing green, toy-like handcuffs. After a quick scan using the Watchtower's atmospheric systems, Cyborg learns the handcuffs are made of an artificial Kryptonite. They're slowly bleeding harmful radiation into the air around Superman.

Cyborg narrows his eyes and clenches his jaw. His friends are in pain. Cyborg's walk turns into a run.

Turn to page 65.

As the cord finishes reeling in and his hand pops back in, Cyborg stands up. He takes a look at his new surroundings.

The training room is a huge chamber that takes up most of this level. It had been worked on recently to add more room, since League training sessions sometimes got out of hand. It's just one side effect of having a team full of mighty superpowered people.

Cyborg spots a man standing right in the center of the large room. "Superman?" he asks.

It is the hero, but the Man of Steel is wearing a mask. A wide smile is frozen onto the doll-like face. The mask is exactly the same as the one worn by the man standing behind the hero.

It's the villain Toyman.

The small man presses a button on the video game controller in his hands. At Toyman's command, Superman flies directly at Cyborg.

WOOOOOSH!

Cyborg barely has time to jump to the side. Superman's attack misses, but he was close enough that Cyborg feels a gush of wind against his face.

If Superman had been moving at full speed, Cyborg would've been flattened into the wall!

Cyborg knows the Man of Steel must be holding back. The mask is obviously some type of mind control device, and Superman is fighting against Toyman's commands. But it's not enough. Cyborg needs to free his teammate completely.

Superman turns back. Through the Toyman mask, he fires a blast of heat vision. Cyborg somersaults out of the way.

The hero's heart is racing, but so is his mind.

If Toyman is controlling Superman by remote control, that means there's a radio signal in the air sending the orders to the mask.

A signal Cyborg can hack.

Turn the page.

Cyborg focuses on his work even as Superman tackles into him. The mind-controlled hero pummels Cyborg's chest. Although the Man of Steel isn't hitting with full strength, Cyborg hears the crunch of his metal torso bending inward.

But he can't deal with that now.

Inside his mind, Cyborg scans the air. Finally, he locks onto the signal he's been looking for. Cyborg concentrates as Superman raises his fist once more.

Just as the Man of Steel is about to strike, he freezes.

Cyborg grins. His hack worked! He's taken over Toyman's remote control signal.

The hero steps away from Superman and faces Toyman. The villain stares at him for a second. Then he runs.

But he doesn't get far. A Batarang suddenly strikes his head, and Toyman falls to the ground.

Batman steps out of the shadows.

"The Joker and the others are in the holding cells," Batman says casually. "They didn't prove to be a problem."

"Seriously?" Cyborg asks as he helps Superman remove the mask. Could Batman have really taken out the entire League of Laughs?

The smile on Superman's face confirms it. He knows his friend well.

"Nice job here," Batman says to Cyborg. Then he leaves the room without another word.

Cyborg gives Superman a puzzled look.

"Hey, that's more than he ever says to me," Superman says.

The Man of Steel flies up the elevator shaft to help with the locked-up villains. Cyborg is glad he's alone, because he can't stop smiling. Batman actually gave him a compliment.

This has been a good day.

THE END

To follow another path, turn to page 13.

Cyborg scans the Batman robot with his palm as the Joker continues to rant through its radio.

"I know what you're thinking, Sparky—can I call you Sparky?" the Joker says, laughing now and then. "You're thinking, it's just the Joker and me. This fight was over before it started!"

Cyborg's electronic eye glows red. His mind is working overtime as it scans the Watchtower systems. The villain can talk all he wants. It's just giving Cyborg time to trace the source of the Joker's broadcast.

"I'm going to agree with you on that point, Tin Man," says the Joker. "No. No, I like Sparky better. Sorry."

But there's something wrong with Cyborg's scan. It's the signal of the broadcast. It's not coming from the Watchtower.

"The fight *is* over, but it's not gonna go the way you're thinking," continues the Joker. "To be honest, I only told Toyman and the others about the Trophy Room because I needed a couple of stooges to distract you and your buddies."

Cyborg continues the trace. But it can't be right. His systems are saying that the Joker is broadcasting from Earth. From Gotham City.

"You see, I was in need of a smile," says the Joker. "I thought, what would make me happier than a good ol' firework show? So I visited your little space clubhouse and planted a few bombs. You have about twenty seconds before you're part of the display, Sparky."

Cyborg doesn't waste any time. He scoops up the unconscious Harley Quinn and Trickster and rushes out of the room. He barely makes it to the Justice League teleporter room before the Watchtower explodes.

The mechanical hero only hopes Batman and Superman were as lucky as he was.

THE END

To follow another path, turn to page 13.

The Joker spins and faces the trapped hero. "Quiet, Bats!" he yells.

But when he turns back around, Toyman isn't there.

"You're right," says Batman. He smiles a rare smile. "I'll be quiet. This isn't my moment."

Before the Joker can reply, a metal fist strikes his nose. The Clown Prince of Crime smacks into the observation window. The force of the impact nearly cracks the thick glass.

"Nah, that's OK, Batman," says Cyborg, stepping out from the shadows. "I don't need the spotlight."

The Joker looks over and spots Toyman slumped on the floor. He manages a single laugh before he too blacks out.

As Cyborg focuses on freeing his teammate, Batman keeps the smile on his face. To Cyborg, that's all the thanks he'll ever need.

THE END

To follow another path, turn to page 13.

As he runs, Cyborg's mind is fast at work. He's connecting to the Watchtower's security system.

Click

"Did you hear that?" Trickster says in the cafeteria. He looks away from Bizarro, who is busy trying to shove an entire cooked chicken into his mouth.

"Bizarro no hear anything," says the pale Superman clone.

"Wait, so does that mean you do hear something, or you don't?" Trickster asks. He shakes his head. "Your backward Bizarro speak makes absolutely no sense to me."

Fssssssssssssssss

"Bizarro no hear that either," says the hulking villain.

"Uh-oh," Trickster says, as he spots the green-tinted gas filling the room.

Two thuds echo in the cafeteria as the villains slump over.

Turn the page.

Cyborg smiles as he watches Trickster and Bizarro pass out on the security video playing inside his mind. It looks like his link with the Watchtower security system is working perfectly.

But he has no time to celebrate the small victory. He's reached the monitor room.

Harley Quinn notices Cyborg standing in the doorway. She turns away from Batman and Superman, who are both still tied up and unconscious.

"Hey!" she says. "Who invited Tin Man?"

"Not me," says the Joker. He pulls a comically large pistol from his pocket. "I'm more of a Dorothy fan myself. I mean, her shoes were to *die* for!"

BLAM!

The Joker fires his gun, but Cyborg has already raced across the room on his superpowered legs. With one punch, the clown flies across the room. He smashes into Harley. The two exchange a polite smile before passing out.

"Not another step," Toyman says. He stands in front of the main console's controls. "I've got the Watchtower heading straight toward Earth. You need me to change the coordinates, unless you want to see this satellite crash into Gotham City."

"Nah," says Cyborg as his arm transforms into his white sound cannon. "I've already reset those coordinates. In fact, I did it before I even came into the room. I've also logged you out of the Watchtower's systems. For good."

Although Cyborg can't tell, he's pretty sure Toyman isn't smiling behind his mask. But it doesn't matter.

Because one sound blast later the villain is out cold. And as Cyborg works on freeing his friends, he knows he's the only person in the Watchtower with a grin on his face.

THE END

To follow another path, turn to page 13.

"So that's what we're doing now?" Cyborg says, watching the robotic tiger that's slowly walking toward him. "We're transforming?"

The hero raises his right arm. "Good to know," he says.

His arm clicks and whirs. As quickly as he can think it, Cyborg's arm transforms into a large, cylinder-like gun. It's a favorite weapon of his— the white sound cannon.

VOOOOOOOMMMM!

The powerful burst of sound smacks straight into the robotic cat. It tumbles backward into a row of elliptical machines. The massive equipment crashes onto the tiger. Sparks spit up from the robot's metal body.

Cyborg gets to his feet. His hand transforms back to normal.

"All right," he says. He flexes his fingers. "What else we got?"

THUNK!

A robotic wolf slams Cyborg into a treadmill.

The mechanical parts that were once the robot's left leg are now a fearsome wolf. It snaps at Cyborg. The hero struggles with the creature, trying to keep its metal fangs away.

"You ruined my tiger," says a voice. It's much creepier than Cyborg remembers.

Toyman steps out of the shadows at the far end of the room. "He was my favorite."

The villain's doll-like mask doesn't move when he speaks. Its bizarre, child-like smile is frozen in place.

"I've always been more of a . . . ugh . . . dog person myself," Cyborg says.

The hero sends nearly all his body's electrical energy into his arms. He uses the extra power to clamp the robotic wolf's jaws shut.

"Well, not this particular dog," Cyborg adds with a smile.

Turn to page 74.

"Batman," whispers Cyborg. "I need you to wake up."

The Dark Knight doesn't respond. Instead, his body begins to tremble. Something seems wrong.

"Batman?" asks Cyborg. "Batman!"

"Stop saying that name already," says Harley Quinn as she enters the room. "How would you like it if I said the same thing over and over?"

Cyborg points. "It's Batman, he's—"

"What did I just tell ya?" says Harley. "Halibut! Halibut!"

The robotic hero blinks. "What?"

"Halibut!" says Harley. "See how annoying that is?"

"You gotta help him!" Cyborg yells as his teammate continues to shake.

"I don't gotta do anything," Harley replies.

She looks down at Batman. The Dark Knight's body twitches again.

"Ah, halibut," she says. "Mr. J will never forgive me if I let Batman kick the bucket before he's done redecorating. Half the fun of winning is lording our victory over dark and gruesome here."

Harley presses a few buttons on the control panel outside Batman's cell. The door opens.

"Look at me!" Harley squeals. "I remembered Toyman's password in one try! What do I win?"

Suddenly, the Dark Knight spins around. His leg sweeps underneath the villain, and she falls down hard. She groans from the floor.

"I would say you win a trip," Batman says as he gets to his feet. "But there have been enough bad jokes for one night."

Cyborg grins. He should've known his friend had a plan. Batman is always prepared.

The Dark Knight stands over Harley. "Now," he says, "I'm going to need the passcodes to the other cells."

Turn to page 79.

It goes against every instinct Cyborg has, but he teleports back up to the Watchtower with Huntress.

After all, Cyborg is new to the Justice League, and Huntress has years of experience. She has to know what's best. Right?

But when the two teleport to inside a prison cell, Cyborg begins to think there is something to that whole "trusting your gut" thing after all.

"Where are we?" Cyborg asks. He doesn't recognize the dark brick walls. "This is most definitely not the Watchtower."

"We're in Arkham Asylum," says Huntress. Her voice is grim. "Arkham Asylum for the Criminally Insane."

"Ding! Ding! Ding!" says a voice through the loudspeakers. "We have a winner."

Cyborg's frown deepens. He knows that voice. It's the Joker.

"You see," the Joker explains, "I wasn't keen on having my shiny new Watchtower infested with you super hero types—"

"Yuck!" Harley Quinn's voice interrupts.

"Not now, Harley!" snaps the Joker. He returns to his usual happy voice and adds, "So I tied up ol' Supes and Bats. Then my friend Toyman reset the coordinates on your teleporters. Hope you've tidied up, because you're about to have a full house!"

Cyborg has heard enough. He transforms his robotic arm into his white sound cannon. He points it at the cell's door. Then he fires.

WEEEEOOOOO!

But the powerful sound waves bounce off the door and right back at the heroes. The force knocks Cyborg and Huntress off their feet.

Huntress groans as she stands back up. "Could you not do that again?" she says to Cyborg.

Turn to page 102.

Cyborg smacks the robot wolf against the hard gym floor. Sparks fly up from it.

Toyman lets out something like a high-pitched scream. The noise is unlike anything Cyborg has ever heard.

But before the hero can respond, a giant robotic hawk and bat dive toward him. Cyborg doesn't move. He stays put as the two flying beasts swoop down.

"Wait for it," Cyborg mumbles to himself. "Wait for it. . . ."

At the last second, Cyborg leaps out of the way using all the strength in his artificial legs.

SMASH!

The robot bat and the robot hawk crash straight into the ground. They explode in a burst of flames.

Turn to page 76.

Cyborg turns toward Toyman. He can't see the villain's expression under that doll-like mask, but it can't be a happy one. Four of his mechanical toys are busted.

However, Toyman doesn't run. Instead, he casually walks over to the last and largest of his robots—the bear.

"You heroes. Always breaking things that don't belong to you," Toyman says as the bear's chest opens. A platform lowers to the floor. "But Joker respects my ideas. That's why he asked me to join the League of Laughs."

"That name really needs work," says Cyborg.

He runs toward the villain, but he's too late. Toyman stepped onto the platform and has been raised into his robot. Cyborg punches at the bear's closed chest, but his metal fists don't even make a dent.

"You bullies always think with your fists," says Toyman. His voice booms through the robot bear's speaker system.

"*We're* the bullies?" Cyborg says. He readies his white sound cannon again. "You attacked us!"

"Oh," says Toyman. The robot bear seems to pause for a moment, as if deep in thought. "I guess we did, didn't we?"

A massive metal paw slams down on Cyborg's shoulder. Then another. Cyborg can't move. He's pinned under the machine. His knees buckle, and he drops to the floor.

"But either way, there's always someone with bigger fists," adds Toyman.

As Cyborg feels the weight of the robot pressing hard against him, he tries to connect to the Watchtower's system again. The Wi-Fi is up, so he quickly sends out an emergency distress signal. He hopes someone notices it.

Before Cyborg blacks out completely, he hears Toyman say, "Goodnight, little toy soldier."

THE END

To follow another path, turn to page 13.

Ten minutes later, Cyborg finds himself hiding in a shadowy corner of the Justice League's monitor room. After Batman freed him, the two locked Harley in a cell and did their best to clean the liquid Kryptonite off Superman. But they couldn't wait for their teammate to recover.

They need to put a stop to the League of Laughs' plans—whatever they are.

Cyborg peeks around the corner. The Joker is looking up at the monitors, laughing at what he sees. Trickster and Toyman are also watching.

Cyborg can't see all of the monitor, but he's certainly curious to know what's captured the villains' attention. The mystery is killing him.

"Look at that!" says the Joker, pointing to the monitor. "That's what I call positive change. Take notes, boys."

"Mm-hmm," says Trickster. He sounds bored. "And how long until he's finished?"

The Joker turns to Trickster. The smile disappears from the clown's face.

Turn the page.

"Ugh, you kids of the smartphone generation," snaps the Joker. "Always wanting everything now, now, now!"

Trickster takes a step back in fear.

"Say, that reminds me. I've been meaning to update my status. . . ." The Joker bursts into his trademark laughter.

Trickster breathes a sigh of relief. He's still alive. For the moment.

"As founding father of the League of Laughs," continues the Joker, "I promised you all a hideout. Now we have one. So let's get to League business, shall—"

TUNK!

A Batarang suddenly smacks into the Joker's head. A second Batarang strikes Trickster. The villains both drop to the floor.

Cyborg barely has time to catch up. He fires his white sound cannon at Toyman.

As soon as the crook slumps over, Cyborg and Batman step out of the shadows.

"Well, that takes care of those guys. But Bizarro's still out there," Cyborg says.

Batman doesn't answer. Instead, he moves to the control panel and starts typing.

Cyborg watches the monitors. Bizarro is hovering outside the Watchtower. The Dark Knight finishes punching in commands. The satellite's hull comes alive with electricity, and the bolts zap the Superman clone. Bizarro's eyes close like a tired toddler before naptime.

"So, new recruit," Batman says to Cyborg. "How are you at buffing out dents?"

Cyborg looks at the monitors again. He finally notices what the Joker had been laughing at. Bizarro has carved a single word into the side of the Watchtower: "Ha."

"Oh man," Cyborg mutters.

Batman smiles. "Welcome to the Justice League."

THE END

To follow another path, turn to page 13.

VOOOOOOOOMMMM!

Cyborg's white sound cannon is as effective as ever. Chunks of concrete shower down from what used to be the ceiling. Cyborg doesn't bother to move. The pieces just bounce off his metal shell.

The hero increases power to his legs and jumps straight up. He lands in the Trophy Room.

"Knock knock," says Cyborg.

Harley Quinn rushes over. She raises a massive mallet, but Cyborg fires his arm cannon before she can strike. The powerful sound pulse knocks Harley off her feet. She smacks into a trophy case and is out cold.

Cyborg quickly looks around. Trickster lies next to the gaping hole, unconscious. The villain must have been near the white sound blast.

Toyman is also knocked out. He's slumped against the wall, and a large boxing glove arrow lies on top of his head. That's what target practice must look like to a crazed clown like the Joker.

The hero readies his sound cannon. He has to focus. The biggest physical threat is still to come. He hasn't dealt with Bizarro yet.

As if on cue, the Superman clone smashes into Cyborg. The hero is sent flying through the room and crashes into a wall.

"Oof," says the Joker from across the large chamber. "That's gonna leave a mark. Or three."

As Cyborg struggles with Bizarro, he catches a glimpse of the Clown Prince of Crime. The villain is picking up the Yellow Lantern Ring from a shattered display case. Cyborg wasn't part of the mission where the League collected that trophy. But he knows it's too dangerous to fall into the Joker's hands.

Unfortunately the hero has other things to worry about. Bizarro has pinned Cyborg against the wall. He slowly starts to crush the hero's metal shell.

"Does this ring make my fingers look fat?" the Joker says as he slips it on. "I'm not—"

Turn the page.

The clown doesn't get to finish his gag. Using every bit of power he can send to his arms, Cyborg whacks Bizarro's jaw. The villain crashes across the room and topples right into the Joker.

"I get it," the Joker says as he drifts into unconsciousness. "Yellow's not . . . my color . . ."

Bizarro isn't defeated as easily. The massive villain gets to his feet and lets out a low growl.

The Superman clones rushes toward Cyborg. But a red beam suddenly blasts into the villain and sends him flying backward.

Cyborg spins around. Behind him stand Superman and Batman. The Man of Steel's eyes glow red with heat-vision. He flies past Cyborg and knocks out Bizarro with a well-timed punch.

The fight is finally over.

"How did you escape . . . ?" Cyborg starts to ask Batman. Then he stops. He already knows the answer. There's a reason they call them the World's Finest Heroes.

The End

To follow another path, turn to page 13.

Five robot animals now face Cyborg from across the gymnasium. Five against one. Cyborg is one of the toughest members of the Justice League, but even he doesn't like those odds.

He came here for Superman, and he's going to find him.

The robotic wolf charges forward. But Cyborg quickly steps out of the gym. He flips the tip of his finger open and shoves his USB drive into the port on the wall panel. He taps into the doors' digital controls.

With a thought, the doors shut tight.

CLANK

The doors close just in time, and the wolf crashes into heavy metal. The doors hold. And so will the doors on the opposite side of the gym. Toyman and his robots won't be going anywhere for a while.

Cyborg lets out a frustrated sigh. Heading to the gym hasn't exactly been a dead end, but it hasn't gotten him any closer to finding Superman either.

Still plugged into the control panel, Cyborg concentrates. He quickly searches through all the Watchtower's cameras and sensors. Maybe there's a new clue to where he should go next.

Nothing. Everything is off-line now.

Usually, the Watchtower is Cyborg's personal playground. It's a high-tech battle station, and the mechanical hero can access its every digital nook and cranny. But if Cyborg is going to find the Man of Steel, he's going to have to do it off-line.

Cyborg unplugs his USB drive from the panel. He increases his voice's speaker and his hearing sensors. This move is dangerous. The extreme focus it takes leaves him open to an attack.

But today, he has no choice.

"Superman?" Cyborg asks. His voice booms like a loudspeaker at a rock concert.

Then he just listens.

Turn the page.

Even if Cyborg hadn't pumped up his volume, Superman should be able to hear him. The Man of Steel has super-hearing, after all. But Cyborg wants to make sure he notices the call.

A moment later, Cyborg's increased hearing sensors pick up a weak whisper.

"I'm . . . here," Superman says.

Cyborg quickly traces Superman's voice. It's coming from the hangar. That's where the Justice League stores their plane, the *Javelin 7*.

After he puts his hearing and voice back to regular settings, Cyborg takes off down the hall. Soon he comes to a stop. He double-checks the Watchtower blueprints stored in his mind. This is the right spot. The hangar is directly below him, one level down.

His hand transforms to his white sound cannon. Cyborg points it at the floor.

Turn to page 96.

Cyborg knows what he must do. He must try to escape.

The hero concentrates, and a series of ones and zeroes appear in his vision. The numbers scroll past in his digital eye. Only he can see the computer code.

With his mind running as fast as the most powerful supercomputer, Cyborg begins his work. The cell is strong enough to hold threats as dangerous as Bizarro, or even Superman. It's so secure that even the most trained escape artists like Batman or Mr. Miracle would have trouble picking the advanced locks.

But Cyborg still has access to his own mind. And his mind is his most dangerous weapon.

Click

He's remotely hacked the security system. And now, just like that, his cell door is wide open.

Turn the page.

BWEEEP! BWEEEP! BWEEEP!

An alarm blares over the loudspeaker.

Cyborg instantly realizes his mistake. He hacked the security system, but Toyman must have already been plugged into it. The villain is almost as skilled as Cyborg with tech. He's probably been watching the hero's every move.

That means Cyborg can't stay in the jail cell holding room. The League of Laughs will be here any second. He can't try to free Batman or Superman. He just doesn't have time.

For now, Cyborg is on his own.

So the hero sends more power to his legs and sprints into the hallway. But as Cyborg races through the Watchtower, the alarm suddenly cuts off. A new sound comes over the loudspeaker.

"You know, I'm trying to have fun here," says a voice. Cyborg instantly recognizes it—the Joker. "But some spoilsport is making it rather difficult."

"You tell 'em, Mr. J!" Harley Quinn's voice chimes in.

"I'd blame Toyman for causing all this trouble. But Harley has already used him for target practice," Joker says.

"Hey, those trick arrows weren't gonna shoot themselves!" Harley adds.

Cyborg stops. Trick arrows? Those weapons are stored in the Trophy Room. The Joker and Harley must be there. It's located one floor above where Cyborg now stands.

"Don't worry, Sparky. She didn't skewer him. Although he will wake up with a splitting headache," says the Joker with a laugh.

The League of Laughs is already turning on each other. How long will it be before they turn their attention to Superman and Batman in the holding cells?

Cyborg looks up at the ceiling. He takes a deep breath.

Turn to page 82.

"Hold on a second," says Cyborg to his teammate. "None of this feels right. Let me check something first."

To Huntress, it looks like Cyborg is staring off into space. But in reality, his mind is racing. At a speed faster than any supercomputer on the planet, his brain pages through Justice League files and security videos.

Suddenly Cyborg's eyes widen. "It's a trap."

"What's a trap?" Huntress asks.

"That distress call," explains Cyborg. "It wasn't from Batman. The Justice League's communication systems are down, and Batman has been unconscious this entire time. Ever since Trickster took him out."

"Trickster?" repeats Huntress. "You're telling me that washed-up crook took down Batman?"

"That fake message went out to the rest of the Justice League," Cyborg says, as if he didn't hear Huntress. "I don't know why, but the Joker wants us all on the Watchtower."

"So we don't do that then," says Huntress.

The way she talks reminds Cyborg of Batman. He briefly wonders if Huntress is trying to be like the Dark Knight. Cyborg thinks she's not quite there yet.

"Got another plan?" Huntress adds.

Cyborg focuses up and looks around the dark alley. "Where are we?"

"Gotham City," says Huntress. She does her best to not roll her eyes.

"OK, so . . . the Gotham Broadcasting Company is nearby," Cyborg says. "It has the most powerful broadcasting system in the city?"

"Well, it probably has the most money," says Huntress. "So, sure."

"Then that's where we need to go," decides Cyborg. He starts walking out toward the street.

"Hey, big guy," says Huntress. "My bike will be quicker."

Turn to page 95.

The motorcycle is just like Huntress—sharp and a little frightening. But Cyborg doesn't have time to admire Huntress' bike. He's busy hanging on for dear life.

"AH!" he exclaims as Huntress whips around another corner.

Huntress shoots back a look. "For a super hero," she says, "you're not that great at keeping your cool."

"For a super hero," Cyborg says through gritted teeth, "you're not that great at obeying traffic laws."

Huntress doesn't respond. Instead she swerves through traffic at eighty miles per hour. She takes a sharp left turn and narrowly avoids crashing into a city bus. When she finally stops, it takes Cyborg a full minute to catch his breath.

"We're here," Huntress says.

Turn to page 103.

WEEEEOOOOOOOO!!!

The cannon's sound blast punches through the metal and concrete floor.

Cyborg drops through the hole and into a corner of the enormous hangar. He dashes behind some stacked crates and readies his cannon for an attack. But no one comes.

Cyborg carefully looks around the crates and out at his new surroundings.

The *Javelin 7* is parked at the end of the hangar. The Joker and Harley Quinn stand nearby. Harley laughs as the Joker spray-paints a large green smile onto the ship.

Behind them Cyborg spots Batman. His teammate is unconscious and trapped in hardened foam. Trickster leans against him, poking at the tough material and giggling.

But the main thing Cyborg notices is the two men fighting in the center of the hangar.

Bizarro has an arm wrapped around the Man of Steel's neck. And the two are tumbling and crashing through the room. No wonder none of the villains noticed Cyborg's entrance.

"Would you keep it down?" the Joker yells at the battling foes. "I'm trying to create art here!"

"Aw, puddin'," Harley chimes in. "You're misunderstood in your own time."

"It's tragic, really," the Joker says.

The situation is as crazy as the Joker himself. Cyborg can't believe the League of Laughs members aren't concerned about the brutal fight happening right in front of them. Judging by the damage done to the room, Bizarro and Superman have been battling for a while.

The brawl is going to end now, if Cyborg has anything to say about it.

He searches through his memory banks, looking for any and all info on Bizarro.

Turn the page.

"Bizarro!" Cyborg yells across the room.

"Oh, great," says the Joker. "Another distraction. Could someone silence that Tin Man?"

Trickster and Harley start running toward Cyborg. The hero ignores them.

"Bizarro!" Cyborg yells again.

The pale-faced Superman clone looks up.

"You've chosen some really good teammates," says Cyborg. "Just look at your pal Joker. He likes you so much, he's smiling."

"Now you're mocking my moneymaker?" says the Joker. "You need better manners, pal."

Bizarro looks from the Joker to Cyborg and back again.

"What a good group of friends," Cyborg says.

"Joker am good guy?" says Bizarro under his breath.

The villain loosens his grip on Superman, but the Man of Steel doesn't act. He waits to see where this goes.

"The best guy," adds Cyborg.

Harley Quinn and Trickster are almost on him now. Harley raises her large, cartoonish mallet. Trickster readies his boxing-glove gun.

But the hero isn't paying any attention to the two villains. He's watching the red blur hurtling straight toward them.

Harley and Trickster are suddenly swept off their feet and sent flying into a nearby wall. They barely have time to groan before they black out.

Bizarro stands over his knocked-out teammates. He turns toward the Clown Prince of Crime.

"Joker and friends am good guys!" Bizarro says with a scowl on his face. "Me crush good guys!"

Cyborg has completely confused the imperfect clone's backward mind. Bizarro flies straight at the League of Laughs leader with his fists raised.

"Uh-oh," says the Joker.

Turn the page.

THUMP!

Superman zooms over and grabs Bizarro's powerful fist just inches in front of Joker's face.

"That'll do," Superman says. He gives Bizarro a polite smile. "I can take it from here."

The Joker lets out a chuckle as he passes out and drops to the floor. The close call was too much for the clown to handle.

By the time the Joker wakes up, Superman and Cyborg have put him in one of the Watchtower's holding cells. The Joker peers through the thick Plexiglas wall. The rest of the League of Laughs is locked up too.

Out of the entire team, only Bizarro seems happy as he scribbles in a ratty old coloring book.

"Oh, so *he* gets artistic license," mutters the Joker.

It's a joke, but not a very good one. Not even the Joker is laughing now.

THE END

To follow another path, turn to page 13.

"Oh," says the Joker over the loudspeaker. "I should mention you're in a high security wing of the Asylum. Those cells can hold the toughest thugs. You won't be leaving anytime soon."

"And the place is empty on account of the repairs it's going through," Harley adds. "That means no guards to find ya and set ya free!"

"Let *them* figure out the joke!" Joker snaps again. "Anyhoo, back to world domination!"

The speaker clicks off.

Huntress looks at Cyborg. They both know this isn't good. Then they hear a buzzing noise. It's the sound of teleporters.

One by one, the cells around them fill with confused members of the Justice League.

"Uh . . . could somebody tell me what's going on?" The Flash asks from a neighboring cell.

But Cyborg and Huntress are too stunned to speak.

THE END

To follow another path, turn to page 13.

Cyborg looks up at the Gotham Broadcasting Company building. With a blink he turns on his infrared vision. He scans the rooftop for body heat signatures. There aren't any.

Cyborg can carry out his plan without interruptions. But first they need to get up there.

The hero steps off the motorcycle and points to his back. "Mind if I take the lead?" he asks.

At first Huntress gives him a curious look, but she then puts her arms around his neck.

POOOOOMMMM

Luckily, Huntress' grip is tight enough when Cyborg's rocket boots activate. The heroes shoot to the top of the building in record time.

"How about a better warning?" Huntress says as she steps onto the rooftop.

Cyborg doesn't apologize. He can't spare another second. Instead he runs over to the Gotham Broadcasting Company's enormous satellite dish. It'll be powerful enough to send a warning message to the League.

Turn the page.

Cyborg rips off the cover on the dish's control panel. The tip of his metal finger flips open to reveal a USB drive. He plugs into the panel.

"Cyborg to Justice League," he says. "Do not use the teleporters. I repeat, do not use the teleporters."

While Cyborg sends out his message, Huntress wanders to the edge of the rooftop. She looks up. A tiny red dot is moving across the nighttime sky. Maybe it's a meteorite?

"The Joker has taken over the Watchtower," Cyborg continues. "Gather forces, but attack from outside. Do not use the teleporters."

Huntress keeps watching the dot. It's getting bigger. "Hey, rookie . . . We may have a problem."

Bizarro suddenly rockets down from the sky straight into the satellite dish.

Cyborg rolls out of the way. He didn't think the League of Laughs would notice his warning this quickly! Bizarro's super-hearing must be just as good as Superman's.

The robotic hero transforms his arm to his white noise cannon. He aims and fires. The imperfect Superman clone yelps as the powerful sound wave smacks into him.

Huntress adds to racket. She readies her crossbow and fires a sonic bolt. It boosts Cyborg's sound blast to extreme levels. Within a second, Bizarro lies on the rooftop, unconscious.

When Cyborg's hearing returns, he notices a beeping in his ear. It's an incoming message.

"Cyborg," says Batman over the comm system. "We're back online up here. Green Lantern and Captain Atom got your warning. They were more than enough to take out Joker and his gang. Nice work."

The mechanical hero turns to Huntress to tell her the good news. But she's already gone.

Cyborg smiles. It looks as if she's more like the Dark Knight than he originally thought.

THE END

To follow another path, turn to page 13.

AUTHOR

The author of the Amazon best-selling hardcover *Batman: A Visual History*, Matthew K. Manning has contributed to many comic books, including *Beware the Batman*, *Spider-Man Unlimited*, *Batman/Teenage Mutant Ninja Turtles Adventures*, *Justice League Adventures*, *Looney Tunes*, and *Scooby Doo, Where Are You?* When not writing comics themselves, Manning often authors books about them, as well as a series of young reader books starring Superman, Batman, and The Flash for Capstone. He currently lives in Asheville, North Carolina, with his wife, Dorothy, and their two daughters, Lillian and Gwendolyn. Visit him online at www.matthewkmanning.com.

ILLUSTRATOR

Erik Doescher is a concept artist for Gearbox Software and a professional illustrator. He attended the School of Visual Arts in New York City and has freelanced for DC Comics for almost twenty years, in addition to many other licensed properties. He lives in Texas with his wife, five kids, two cats, and two fish.

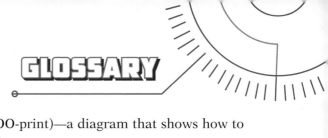

GLOSSARY

blueprint (BLOO-print)—a diagram that shows how to make something

clone (KLOHN)—an exact copy of a person or thing

console (KOHN-sohl)—a panel that has controls for a machine or electronic equipment

coordinates (koh-AWR-duh-nits)—measurements used to mark an exact spot on Earth or in space

electromagnetic pulse (i-lek-troh-mag-NET-ik PUHLS)—a burst of energy that damages electronic equipment

hack (HAK)—to break into and use a computer network without permission

hangar (HANG-ur)—an area where aircraft are stored

infrared vision (in-fruh-RED VIZH-uhn)—being able to see things by the heat they give off

navigation (NAV-uh-gay-shun)—having to do with the process that moves a vessel from one place to another

satellite (SAT-uh-lite)—a spacecraft that circles Earth

sensor (SEN-sur)—a device that can notice changes in heat, light, sound, or motion

teleport (TEL-uh-pawrt)—to move from one place to another instantly

unconscious (uhn-KON-shuhss)—not awake; being unconscious is often because of an injury or drug

THE JOKER

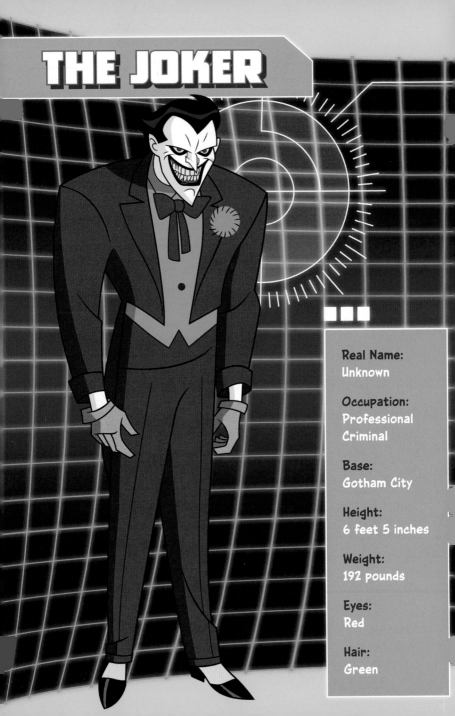

Real Name:
Unknown

Occupation:
Professional
Criminal

Base:
Gotham City

Height:
6 feet 5 inches

Weight:
192 pounds

Eyes:
Red

Hair:
Green

The Clown Prince of Crime. The Ace of Knaves. Batman's most dangerous enemy is known by many names, but he answers to no one. After falling into a vat of toxic waste, this once lowly criminal was transformed into an evil madman. The chemical bath bleached his skin, dyed his hair green, and peeled back his lips into a permanent grin. Since then, the Joker has had only one purpose in life . . . to destroy Batman. In the meantime, however, he's happy tormenting the good people of Gotham City.

- The Joker always wants the last laugh. To get it, he's planned dozens of deadly clown tricks. He has even gone as far as faking his own death!

- Always the trickster, the Joker designs all of his weapons to look comical in order to hide their true danger. This trickery usually gets a chuckle or two from his foes, giving the Joker an opportunity to strike first.

- The Clown Prince of Crime has spent more time in Arkham Asylum than any Gotham criminal. But that doesn't mean he's comfortable behind bars. He has also escaped more times than anyone.

- While at Arkham, the Joker met Dr. Harleen Quinzel. She fell madly in love and helped the crazy clown in his many escapes. Soon, she turned to a life of crime herself, as the evil jester Harley Quinn.

STRENGTH IN NUMBERS

12 POSSIBLE ENDINGS

THE ULTIMATE WEAPON
BY MATTHEW K. MANNING

12 POSSIBLE ENDINGS

THE LEAGUE OF LAUGHS
BY MATTHEW K. MANNING

12 POSSIBLE ENDINGS

THE PORTAL OF DOOM
BY LAURIE S. SUTTON

12 POSSIBLE ENDINGS

COSMIC CONQUEST
BY LAURIE S. SUTTON

ONLY FROM capstone